The Odd Puppy

LEETRESS M. BURRIS

PAGE PUBLISHING, INC.
Conneaut Lake, PA

First originally published by Page Publishing 2020

ISBN 978-1-68456-822-2 (pbk)
ISBN 978-1-68456-823-9 (digital)

Printed in the United States of America

To All Children,

It is okay to be different. You are you and I am me and that's the way we are meant to be. You are SOMEBODY special! Just love yourself.

Leetress M. Burris

Once upon a time, a mother dog had five little puppies. She had two girl and three boy puppies. The older four puppies looked alike. They were black and white and had long tails and were the same size. The youngest puppy was small, brown, and had a short tail. He was the runt of the litter. The mother dog loved all of her puppies and was so proud of them.

But her motherly instincts told her that her youngest would have some trouble in his young life. So she named him Oddball. Oddball loved to stay close to his mother while his brothers and sisters began to find their way and play in the grass.

"Come on, Oddball!" they would shout. "Let's play tag."

As soon as Oddball left from his mother's side and started joining in the fun, he would trip over his feet. His brothers and sisters would laugh at him.

When it was time to eat, his brothers and sisters rushed to gobble their food, and by the time Oddball got there, the food would be gone.

5

When the mother dog would teach her young puppies the ways of puppy life, such as barking, growling, and sniffing, the other pups "barked," "growled," and "sniffed" on command. But Oddball had a hard time doing his dog duties. Again, his brothers and sisters would laugh at him.

The mother said to her pups, "It's not nice to make fun of your brother or others. Everybody learns in their own time."

After several months, the puppies were big enough and ready to go to a new home. Little children with their moms and dads picked up and played with the other puppies. Oddball stayed near his mother.

"Go on, son! You will find a nice home too."

Oddball tried going out and showing his best dog face and tricks, but one little girl said, "That puppy looks different. He is not cute at all."

Everyone seemed to ignore Oddball.

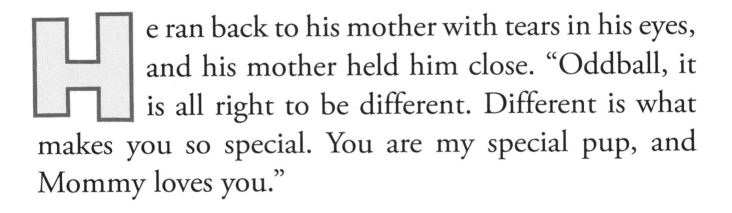

He ran back to his mother with tears in his eyes, and his mother held him close. "Oddball, it is all right to be different. Different is what makes you so special. You are my special pup, and Mommy loves you."

All of his brothers and sisters found new homes that day. Oddball and his mother stayed together. As Oddball grew older, he began to change.

His brown fur became thick and glossy. He could glide over the grass with his long strides barking, playing, growling, and sniffing. He became a protector and a most handsome canine.

One day, the little girl who had come to pick up one of his brothers months before came by with her father on the farm.

She wondered where was the odd-looking puppy that she had seen before. She saw the mother dog and then she saw the most good-looking dog standing beside her. The little girl ran to her father and told him that is the kind of dog she wanted. She called Oddball by saying, "Come here, boy!"

Oddball looked at the little girl because he remembered her. He hesitated. Oddball's mother told him, "It's all right, son. It's your time. Just go over and be yourself."

Oddball slowly walked over to the little girl and sat down in front of her. The little girl said, "You are the most beautiful dog I have ever seen." She went to Oddball and hugged him and then looked at her father. "Dad, can I take him home with me?"

Her father said, "I'll see what I can do. I need to ask the farmer if he is for sale."

The father went to talk to the farmer about Oddball. Then her father came over and said, "Yes, if he is what you want, then we can take him home."

"Yippee!" the little girl exclaimed.

Oddball looked at his mother, and she had tears in her eyes. "Son, be happy. The little girl has chosen well. You have come into your own. I love you and enjoy your life."

Oddball went to his mother and gave her a goodbye kiss. Then he said, "Mom, thank you for everything. I will miss you so much, and I love you." Then he wagged his tail and ran to his little girl.

ddball missed his mother throughout his life, but he lived happily for the rest of his days with his new family.

20

About the Author

Leetress M. Burris developed a love for writing at a very early age. Her journey began with reading books from the library that her mother worked. She discovered that she could go anywhere in a book by using her imagination. This led her to write poetry, short stories, and eventually, her first book. Ms. Burris is an elementary school teacher and resides in Delaware. She enjoys spending time with her family including her four-legged furry child, Snuggles, attending church services, reading, writing, and traveling. She has several books published: *A Wish for Snuggles*, *Heroes of the Bible: The Stories of Joseph, Noah, and Jonah*, *Maps Are Amazing!*, *I Am Me!* and *The Odd Puppy*.

CPSIA information can be obtained
at www.ICGtesting.com
Printed in the USA
LVHW071501270722
724460LV00013B/226